The Magical Hair Bows

by Terrie Lynn Birney

Illustrated by Solomiia at GetYourBookIllustrations

Dreams really come true
#tmhb
#mydreamcametrue

DEDICATION

To my loving mother, who is the best mama in the world
and who I love bunches!

To my loving and supportive husband,
thank you for supporting me through
this crazy experience! I love you very much!

To my cousin, Pattie, thank you for helping me
with writing this book! I love you!

To my writing coach, Karen Ferreria,
I couldn't have done this without you. Thank you!

ISBN: 978-1-957696-04-1   (Ebook)
ISBN: 978-1-957696-05-8   (Hardback)
ISBN: 978-1-957696-06-5   (Paperback)

Illustrated by Solomiia at GetYourBookIllustrations
Book and Cover Design by Kezia at GetYourBookIllustrations
www.getyourbookillustrations.com

First Print 2023

Publisher's Cataloging-in-Publication Data provided by Five Rainbows Cataloging Services
Names: Birney, Terrie Lynn, author. | Solomiia, illustrator.
Title: The magical hair bows / Terrie Lynn Birney ; Solomiia, illustrator.
Description: Newport, NC : Birney's Books Company, 2023. | Summary: Angel, a little girl with Cerebral Palsy finds a magical
ribbon that change her life. | Audience: Grades pre-K to 7.
Identifiers: ISBN 978-1-957696-05-8 (hardcover) | ISBN 978-1-957696-06-5 (paperback) | ISBN 978-1-957696-04-1 (ebook)
Subjects: LCSH: Picture books for children. | High interest-low vocabulary books. | CYAC: Cerebral palsy--Fiction. | Friendship-
-Fiction. | Families--Fiction. | Fairy tales. | BISAC: JUVENILE FICTION / Disabilities & Special Needs. | JUVENILE FICTION /
Social Themes / Friendship. | JUVENILE FICTION / Fairy Tales & Folklore / General. | JUVENILE FICTION / Readers / Beginner.
Classification: LCC PZ7.1.B56 Ma 2023 (print) | LCC PZ7.1.B56 (ebook) | DDC [E]--dc23.

I love spending time with my family and friends and playing in the park with my puppy, Chocolate!

Hi! My name is Angel! I have Cerebral Palsy.

That means that I can't talk or walk as the other kids do.
When I try to get up out of my wheelchair and walk, I flop down every time.

I also try to talk, but no words come out of my mouth.
Just a weird sound like "Hon".

I have my special language with my close friends and family: sign language.
And I get to sit in a cool ride, a wheelchair.

One day after school, I was playing with my puppy Chocolate
and our neighbor, Rosie, in my backyard.

Chocolate was chasing us, and he got stuck in the fence. I tried to
pull him out, but my wheelchair just spun around and around.

Rosie said, "Angel, it's alright,
I will save him!"

I signed to my best friend, "But I
just wish I could help my friends
and family like y'all help me!"

"I LOVE YOU, ROSIE!"

"I LOVE YOU TOO, ANGEL!"

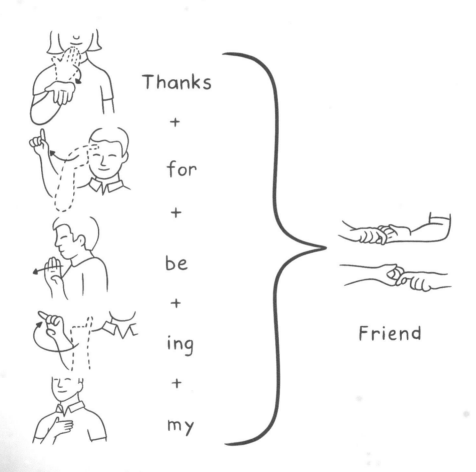

Thanks

+

for

+

be

+

ing

+

my

Friend

Mama and I were taking
Chocolate for a walk in the park.
Some kids were playing on swings.
And as I watched, I wished I could
play with them so badly.

As we passed by the swings, something caught my eye. I asked Mama to hand it to me. Mama said, "Angel, wow, it is a ribbon, and it is the Cerebral Palsy support color, *green!*"

While I was holding the ribbon in my hand,
I looked up at the sky and thought to myself:

I WISH I COULD WALK AND TALK!

The ribbon twinkled in my hand as I looked down at it.
I felt my legs and arms getting stronger,

I jumped out of my wheelchair
and ran with Chocolate and yelled,
"I can run!" and whispered,
"Oh, I'm talking!

We started jumping up and down and
I picked up Chocolate and danced with
him in my arms and sang the song,

"Green Ribbon,
Green Ribbon"

THUD!

When we got home, Rosie came over to play and I told her about the ribbon. I signed, "I can walk and talk if I hold on to the ribbon."

Rosie said, "Angel, a little ribbon can't make you walk and talk, Silly Head!" I looked down at my hand, and the ribbon was gone.

"Uh-huh, Rosie, we will find it and you will see!" I made a yelling sound and Mama shouted, "Oh no, where could it be?!"

The three of us looked everywhere for the special ribbon.

Mama said, "Sweetheart, it'll be alright. We'll find it!". I signed, "But if the magical ribbon is gone forever, I can't run with my friends!".

"Oh, my sweet Angel, we will find it,"
Mama said, "But if we don't, it won't
be the end of the world. I love you
just the way you are!"

I signed. "I know, but I want to run
with my friends and Chocolate!"

We finally found the ribbon; Chocolate
was playing with it on my bed.

So, Mama made two hair bows out of the ribbon and put them in my ponytails. I touched both bows and wished that I could walk and talk.

I sprung out of my wheelchair and dashed to Mama.

I gave her the biggest hug ever and yelled,
"I love you bunches, Mama!

You are the best Mama in the world!"

"Rosie, na-na-na-na-na, I told
you so. With the sparkling
magical hair bows in my hair,
I can walk and talk!"

Later, I was playing with Rosie and Chocolate. Chocolate found a bone and started to bury it, but he dug a hole that was too big.

CLONK!

"Rosie, since I have my special bows in my hair,
I'll go down and get Chocolate!"

I jumped into the hole, carrying out my sweet
Chocolate in my arms.

I love being able to run and play with all my friends and Chocolate.

I also enjoy dancing while I'm singing
my favorite songs, especially the song
"Green Ribbon, Green Ribbon".

Being able to tell mama how much I love her is the thing I love doing most of all!

10 FUN FACTS ABOUT SIGN LANGUAGE

1. IT'S FAIRLY POPULAR IN AMERICA

In America alone, there are just under 1 million people that are deaf or hearing impaired or about 3.6% of the population. It's thought that up to 2 million people speak American Sign Language. ASL is the fifth most common language spoken in America, behind English, Spanish, Italian, German, and French. How about that as one of the top ASL facts for you there!

2. IT'S SO EASY THAT A MONKEY CAN DO IT

Well, maybe sign language isn't that easy. It is a complex language. However, both monkeys and babies have been able to learn simple sign language. Children learn sign language in the same general pattern they learn to speak. First, babies will start with simple signs or incorrect symbols that represent a word as they get older, they refine their sign language and the motions become more correct.

3. AMERICAN SIGN LANGUAGE ISN'T ONLY FOR DEAF PEOPLE

People who can't speak use sign language to communicate with their loved ones, like the author of this book, Terrie Lynn Birney, and her main character, Angel.

4. IT'S A SECRET LANGUAGE

American Sign Language could be a secret and fun language between friends. Imagine you and your BBF want to your secrets or feelings with only each other, then ASL is the key. So, learning American Sign Language as a child and that fun hobby will probably be handy for the rest of your life.

5. IT'S PART OF BASEBALL

If you have ever watched or played baseball, you have likely noticed that coaches and players communicate on the field with signs. This practice is because of a deaf player on the Chicago White Sox, William Hoy. Since he couldn't hear the umpire's calls, Hoy and his coach came up with a series of signals to pass the calls on. Over time, this caught on with other players and teams. Now, teams across all sports use sign language as a secret way to communicate! However, it isn't ASL, really.

6. NAMES HAVE A SIGN

Rather than spell out a name, people have a sign that represents their name. When you meet a new person who speaks sign language, it is common practice to exchange how to sign one's name as an introduction.

7. LEARNING SIGN LANGUAGE IS GOOD FOR YOUR BRAIN

It's no secret that learning a second language is beneficial to brain function. Science tells us speaking at least two languages improves memory, increases problem-solving skills and critical thinking, enhances concentration, and increases one's ability to multitask.

8. SIGN LANGUAGE IS QUITE COMMON

In the world, over 70 million people use a version of sign language as their primary means of communication. And over 150 million people throughout the world use sign language to communicate with friends or family members that are hearing impaired.

9. BRAIN INJURIES AFFECT THE ABILITY TO SIGN

Just like an injury to one's brain, either from trauma or stroke can affect their ability to speak words, it can also affect their ability to speak in sign language. Brain injury sufferers must often learn to sign again through therapy.

10. SIGNS ARE FEMININE OR MASCULINE

Just like in many spoken languages, there are different signs to refer to gender. In American Sign Language, speakers sign words and terms referring to women near the speaker's jaw. However, when one speaks about a man, one makes the signs near their forehead.

FACTS ABOUT CEREBRAL PALSY
DID YOU KNOW…?

Cerebral Palsy is the Most Common Childhood Motor Disability

Cerebral palsy is an umbrella term, meaning that it describes a wide range of motor impairments at various severities. As a result, every case of cerebral palsy is unique and requires a personal management. Individuals with Cerebral Palsy Can Improve Motor Functions Cerebral palsy is a lifelong condition, meaning that the brain damage that causes it will not go away. However, the brain has neuroplasticity, which is the ability to rewire itself and reassign affected functions to undamaged areas of the brain. Through intensive training that focuses on high repetitions, individuals with cerebral palsy can promote neuroplasticity and improve their motor functions. Early intervention is key to improving motor functions because children's brains have greater levels of plasticity than adult brains.

Cerebral Palsy is Not Hereditary

Cerebral palsy is not hereditary, so the chance of an adult with cerebral palsy passing the motor disability down to their child is the same as an adult without cerebral palsy.

· Rather, the following can cause Cerebral Palsy:
· bleeding in the brain
· infections
· seizures
· premature birth
· traumatic injury to the head

There are 4 different types of Cerebral Palsy:

We can classify cerebral palsy into 4 different types:

· Spastic (characterized by stiff movements and caused by damage to the motor cortex)
· Dyskinetic (characterized by uncontrollable movements and caused by damage to the basal ganglia)
· Ataxic (characterized by poor balance and coordination and caused by damage to the cerebellum)
· Mixed (a combination of 2 or more types of CP)

You Cannot Get Cerebral Palsy as an Adult

Cerebral palsy is a motor disability caused by damage to the brain before or during birth, or shortly after birth. Sometimes, milder forms of cerebral palsy may go unnoticed until the child shows developmental delays. The doctors do not consider any sort of motor disability that occurs in later childhood or adulthood cerebral palsy. Similarly, you cannot "catch" cerebral palsy at any age; it is not contagious.

Cerebral Palsy Does Not Affect a person's intellectual, but sometimes

Cerebral palsy is a motor disorder, meaning that it specifically affects movement. Some people with Cerebral Palsy are as intelligent as anyone else, like the author of this book, Terrie Lynn Birney, and her main character, Angel.

NATIONAL AWARENESS DATES & OTHER INTERESTING INFORMATION

Cerebral Palsy Awareness color is GREEN, mostly LIGHT GREEN

National Tell a Fairy Tale Day is FEBRUARY 26TH

Cerebral Palsy Awareness Month is MARCH

National American Sign Language Day is MARCH 15TH

National Fairy Tale Day is MAY 3RD

National Girlfriends Awareness Day is AUGUST 1ST

Cerebral Palsy Awareness Day is OCTOBER 6TH

National Green Day is OCTOBER 17TH

National Magic Date is OCTOBER 31ST

ABOUT THE AUTHOR

As a child with Cerebral Palsy, Terrie Lynn Birney never saw a book about someone like her. She had an idea for a children's book and enjoyed writing since she can remember, but it was not until last year, she started taking her joy of writing seriously and made her dream to publish come true! She took an amazing Children's Book Mastery writing coaching program. That program led her to writing and publishing her first book, "The Magical Hair Bows". Terrie Lynn believes that this book, "The Magical Hair Bows" is a wonderful fairy tale not only for children with Cerebral Palsy, but it also teaches other children that people who have Cerebral Palsy are like anyone else. Terrie Lynn lives in North Carolina with her loving husband of twenty-eight years. She enjoys spending time with her family and finds comfort and pride in being a Christian. She graduated with her associate degree in computer science in 1994.

JOIN MY NEWSLETTER LIST

and receive an exclusive coloring sheet of Angel, Rosie, Mama, and Chocolate. or an original song about Angel's first adventure. Visit my website, www.terrielynnbirneyauthor.com for the freebies and more information.

Look for my second book this fall.
"The Fishing Buddies" is
the first book in the series,
"The Buddies"
It will be available for
pre-order this summer.
For more information, scan
the QR code:

Printed in the USA
CPSIA information can be obtained
at www.ICGtesting.com
LVHW061405210923
757698LV00004B/6